Kitty
Princess
and the
Newspaper Dress

EMMA CARLOW
AND
TREVOR DICKINSON

CANDLEWICK PRESS
CAMBRIDGE, MASSACHUSETTS

For Ella and Lucy.

A special thanks to Jo for all her help and encouragement,
and also for being such a brilliant Fairy Godmouse.

T.D.

For my dear grandmas.

E.C.

First U.S. edition 2003

First published in Great Britain in 2003 by Orchard Books, London

Library of Congress Cataloging-in-Publication Data is available.
Library of Congress Catalog Card Number 2002031155

ISBN 0-7636-2077-7

2 4 6 8 10 9 7 5 3 1

Printed in Belgium

This book was typeset in Cygnet.
The illustrations were done in collage: paper, cloth, crayon, lace,
and other media, including a freshly fried egg.

Candlewick Press
2067 Massachusetts Avenue
Cambridge, Massachusetts 02140

visit us at www.candlewick.com

Meet Kitty Princess.
She likes to think she's the cutest kitty in town.
But once upon a time she was the rudest.

When Kitty Princess wanted something, would she say *please*? Oh, no. **"THAT'S AN ORDER!"** she would shout. And when she got what she wanted, she never ever said *thank you.*

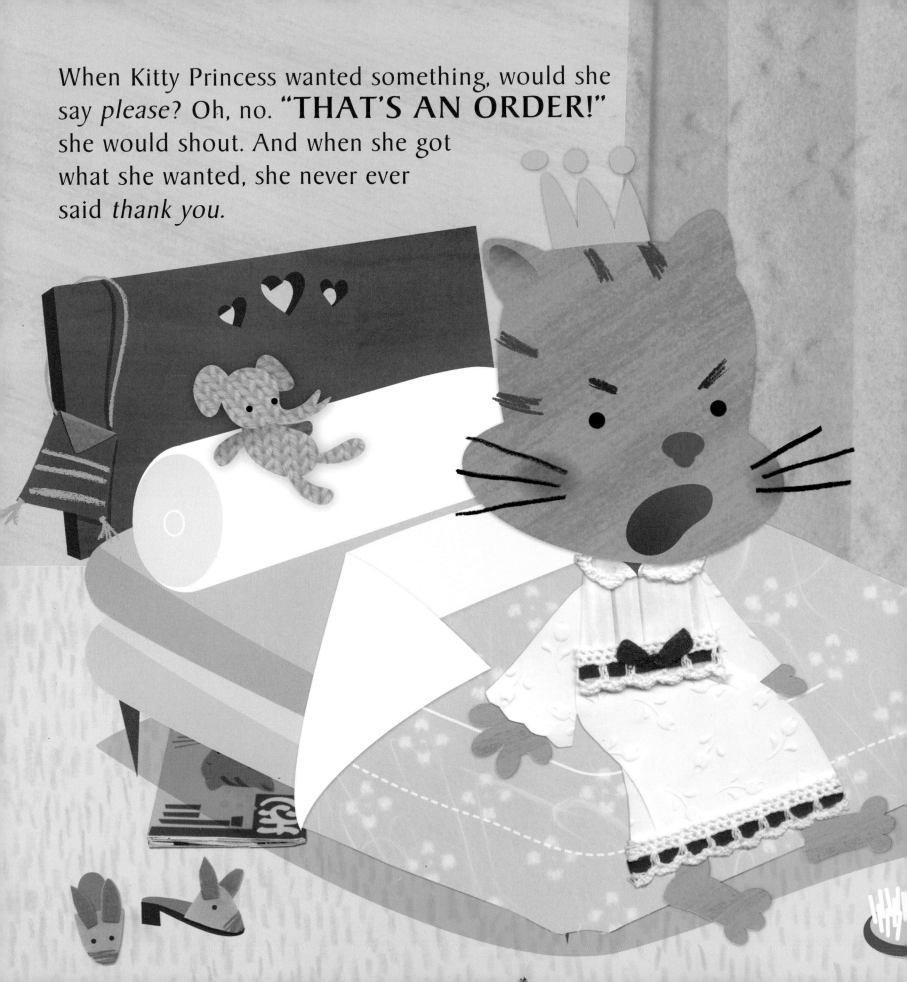

My name is Fairy Godmouse. I take care of Kitty Princess. I've always been patient, loving, and kind—if I do say so myself. But Kitty was so rude sometimes, even I couldn't take it.

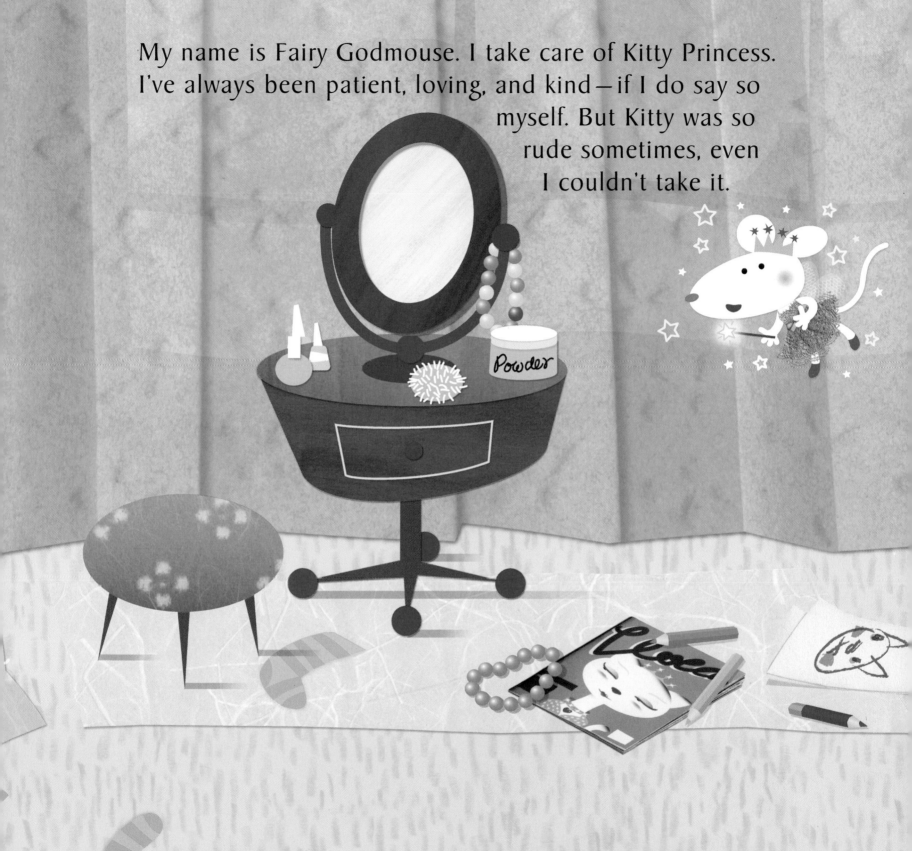

Like the morning she woke me up, shouting . . .

"GET ME THE BEST DRESS IN THE WORLD FOR PRINCE QUINCE'S BALL TONIGHT. AND THAT'S AN ORDER!"

Well, I tried my best,
but my mousy magic isn't
so hot before breakfast.

"Your spells are pathetic," proclaimed Kitty.
"I could do better myself."

"Kitty Princess, you are being very rude,"
I told her. "Please say you're sorry."

"No," said Kitty. "Won't."

"Well, perhaps you should try getting your
own dress," I said.

"Fine!" said Kitty. "That's easy. Just watch me!"

So Kitty stomped into town. I followed at a safe distance so Kitty wouldn't see me.

Since she'd never been shopping before,
I thought it might be interesting to watch.

VEGETABLES

Kitty went into the first store she saw
to buy some shoes.

"Make me a pair of your prettiest shoes by dinnertime," demanded Kitty.

"But madam, we only sell fruits and vegetables," cried the owner.

Kitty wouldn't listen.

"Shoes by dinnertime, **OR ELSE. THAT'S AN ORDER!**" And she swept out of the store.

Next, Kitty went into a café. "Make me your most precious jewelry by dinnertime!" she shouted.

"I'm sorry, did you say *jewelry*?" asked the waitress.

"*What else would I be asking for?*" hissed Kitty.

"But miss—" the waitress tried to reply.

"**THAT'S AN ORDER!**" yelled Kitty.

Last of all, Kitty marched up to the newsstand.

"Make me **THE BEST DRESS IN THE WORLD** by dinnertime!" she commanded.

"But we only have newspapers and magazines here," answered the salesman.

"THAT'S AN ORDER!" shouted Kitty Princess, and she stormed away.

At dinnertime, Kitty pranced back into town.
She was looking forward to being the
cutest princess at the party . . .

but she was in for a **BIG** surprise.

She went into the market. "Here are your shoes, madam,"
said the owner. "Just as you ordered."

"What?" cried Kitty. But there was no time to argue—
the ball was about to start.

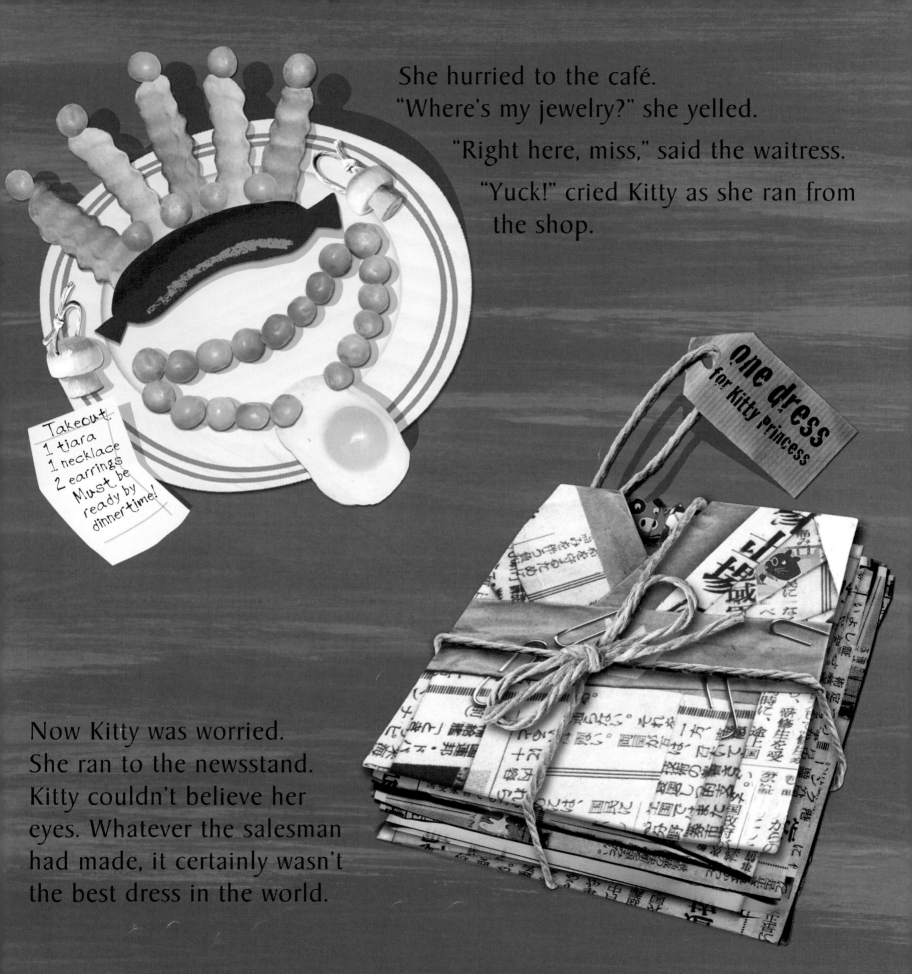

She hurried to the café.
"Where's my jewelry?" she yelled.

"Right here, miss," said the waitress.

"Yuck!" cried Kitty as she ran from the shop.

Takeout
1 tiara
1 necklace
2 earrings
Must be
ready by
dinnertime!

One dress
for Kitty Princess

Now Kitty was worried.
She ran to the newsstand.
Kitty couldn't believe her
eyes. Whatever the salesman
had made, it certainly wasn't
the best dress in the world.

When Kitty Princess got home, she put on her party outfit. She didn't look pretty. She just looked plain silly, but there was no time to make a new outfit. Kitty would have to go to the ball wearing the worst dress in the world.

When she arrived at Prince Quince's palace, the butler would not let her in.

"I have never seen anyone dressed so ridiculously in my entire life," he said. "I simply cannot allow you to enter."

But everyone else was going to the ball—
the owner of the market, the waitress,
and even the newspaper man.

Everyone but Kitty.

Kitty Princess didn't know what to do.
Everything had gone wrong.
Kitty looked very sad indeed.

"FAIRY GODMOUSE, PLEASE COME BACK.
I'M SORRY!"

Did you hear that? Kitty Princess actually said "I'm sorry!"
I decided to make an appearance.

"Oh, Fairy Godmouse, I'll never call your spells pathetic again.
From now on I'll try to be a much nicer princess."

I gave her a kiss and said,
"Is there anyone else you
should be saying *sorry* to?"

"Well," sniffed Kitty, "I'm sorry for being rude to the owner of the market." And as she said *sorry*, her vegetable shoes turned into the prettiest and most dazzling slippers.

Everyone gasped.

"I'm sorry to you too, Waitress," she said.
And Kitty Princess's nasty jewelry turned into the
most exquisite and precious jewelry ever seen.

Everyone ooohed.

"And I'm very sorry to you as well, Newspaper Man," cried Kitty. And no sooner had the words left her lips than her newspaper dress changed into THE BEST DRESS IN THE WHOLE WORLD!

Everyone aaahed.

"Thank you, Fairy Godmouse!" whispered
Kitty as the butler ushered her into the ball.

Kitty looked beautiful—
if I do say so myself.
So beautiful, in fact, that
Prince Quince marched
straight up to her and said . . .

So I turned him into a frog!